WILD BOY

by THOMAS FALL

Illustrated by Leo Summers

SCHOLASTIC BOOK SERVICES

NEW YORK • TORONTO • LONDON • AUCKLAND • SYDNEY

Text copyrght © 1965 by Thomas Fall. Illustrations copyright
© 1968 by Scholastic Magazines, Inc. This edition is published
by Scholastic Book Services, a division of Scholastic Magazines,
Inc., by arrangement with The Dial Press, Inc.

1st printing .... December 1968

Printed in the U.S.A.

For
Ian Kirkpatrick

On the Wild Horse Desert

of West Texas, 1870

"WE will rest for a few minutes, Grandfather," Roberto said. "Then you will be all right."

"Yes, Roberto—for a few minutes," his grandfather replied through lips so parched they could scarcely move. The boy and his grandfather were sitting in the dusty grass near a prairie dog mound. One of the old man's eyes was closed and the other seemed as faded as fog at daybreak. Through it he looked up at Roberto quietly.

Pity for his grandfather surged in Roberto's heart. He wondered desperately if the best plan would be to leave the old man here and go alone on one of the mules in search of water, or to continue coaxing his grandfather along.

The sun beat down unmercifully. Roberto took the packs from the backs of their mules and set them beside his grandfather. He noticed the old man's lips move as though to speak.

Roberto leaned over and said, "Don't try to talk for awhile. We must rest. Even Plato is tired," he added, glancing at the mule his grandfather had been riding. The mule's ears lay back for an instant at the sound of its name.

Roberto searched the endless horizon for an idea. Toward the northeast he might, if he were lucky, find a cavalry detachment. A band of Comanche Indians had told them on the trail three days ago that a platoon of U.S. Cavalry troops from Fort Mystic had recently established a temporary quarters west of the escarpments, at the edge of the high plains. But could his grandfather survive being left alone in the hot sun while he searched for the troops?

He looked to the southwest. In the far distance the blue haze of mountains identified his position. Those mountains had guided generations of Indian warriors along the Comanche Trail of west Texas, and Roberto had learned much from the Comanches. He knew that he was more than a day away from water in that direction.

He looked down at his grandfather and realized that he must decide immediately.

"Grandfather, listen to me," he said. "I am going to leave you and try to find the cavalry encampment. Can you hear me?"

His grandfather nodded and said, "Take Plato. Even though he looks tired, he can go without water longer than Socrates." Socrates was the mule Roberto had been riding. "If darkness overtakes you, stop until daylight. You will never find your way through the prairies at night."

"Lie still and rest, Grandfather. . . ."

Roberto dug into the packs beside the mules and found wooden stakes to which he picketed the animals each night when there was no tree nearby. He split the stakes in half with the sharp edge of a spade—one of the few tools they had brought with them when they gave up the quest for gold in New Mexico. He spread out his blanket on the grass and drove splinters of the stakes into the ground at its corners. He tied the blanket securely with a thong. It was an Indian blanket, brightly striped. Now the wind could not blow it away; stretched out between the stakes, it would be visible from a long distance when he returned looking for his grandfather—if he returned during daylight.

He hobbled Socrates, the mule he was leaving behind, so it could not stray far. Then he slung two empty canteens over Plato's shoulders and hopped on the animal bareback.

Carefully taking his direction from the mountains, he rode directly northeast. He knew that unless he kept accurate bearings he would never be able to find his grandfather again, even with the help of the Indian blanket.

A herd of wild mustangs thundered across the prairie far ahead of him, raising a dust cloud that gradually moved, shimmering in the heat, toward the eastern horizon. A feeling of great excitement swelled in his heart, but he told himself that he would never have anything to do with wild horses again. His father had been killed trying to catch them, and his grandfather had said, "I am too old to chase wild horses and you are too young, Roberto. We will search for gold instead."

Now he must not think of the mustangs, nor even watch them, lest he lose his location. He looked straight ahead, toward the northeast, and urged Plato on. When the mule became tired, Roberto walked for a while, leading the animal to let it rest from its burden. The only thing he feared was that his grandfather might die before he could return with water.

Chapter Two

ROBERTO's heart leaped when he saw another dust trail just before dark. It was not on the eastern horizon, but toward the north. And it was not a billowing cloud of dust, rising into the sky from the turbulence of pounding mustang hoofs. It was a thin, powdery line, like brownish smoke, that could only have been made by the cavalry troops.

He stopped to study the horizon in every direction: he would alter his course now, and he must be sure of his position. In the west the setting sun had left the sky aflame with orange and purple streaks which cast reflections on the desert floor. The blue-hazed mountains, now far to the southwest, were bathed in a delicate orange glow.

He turned back toward the thin dust line and started walking fast, once more leading the mule. "It will be dark very soon, Plato," he said to the animal. "We must hurry."

The mule's ears lay back as though it understood.

Twilight came before Roberto reached the cavalry campsite, but the campfires guided him as he hurried on. Although his legs were weary and his mouth was dry as thistledown, he scarcely noticed. His only concern was that he might not be able to convince the soldiers that he could lead them to his grandfather at night. As well trained as the soldiers were, they did not know as much as he knew about the desert, for he had lived on the desert and the surrounding prairies all his life.

Suddenly, as he drew closer to the campfires, an idea came to him. He stopped and said quietly to the mule, "Plato, please forgive me. I will come back for you in a little while." He hobbled the mule's front feet with the bridle. "You would follow me if you could. I think I had better take no chances. The soldiers will never listen to a boy; they will think I am crazed with thirst. It will be safer if I steal some water from them and hurry back to Grandfather alone."

He walked silently, searching the darkness for the sentry who he knew would be riding in a wide circle around the encampment. At last he lay on his stomach and crawled slowly forward, pausing after each movement to listen. The troopers were telling jokes and laughing as they kindled fires to roast their meat and boil their coffee. Suddenly he heard hoofs in the grass nearby. It was the sentry approaching. He lay as still as a rabbit in the brush, and the sentry passed.

He crawled closer, then flattened himself behind a hummock of buffalo grass and stared around the camp until he spied the water canteens. Stretched out in a line near them were the cavalry saddles, saddlebags, and bedrolls. Beyond the saddles, two hundred feet from the campsite, the cavalry horses quietly grazed, stamping occasionally and snorting with contentment.

It might just be possible, Roberto thought, *for me to approach from the direction of the saddles. I could hide behind them while the soldiers are eating and take a canteen. And maybe even one of the saddlebags—they will contain food.*

He pushed away from the hummock where he lay and inched backward out of the firelight's glow. He circled silently to the opposite side of the camp. Once more he lay still until the sentry passed. And after he found the position he wanted, with the saddles and bedrolls in front of him, he waited for the soldiers to eat.

"Hey, Corporal," said one of the soldiers, "is that buffalo meat or horse meat you're eating tonight?"

"That's steer meat, same as yours!" said the corporal.

"I wouldn't care if mine was wolf, or even wild-cat!" cried another soldier. "I'm hungry enough to eat anything."

The smell of roasting smoked meat, mixed with the aroma of boiling coffee, reached Roberto. Nothing had ever smelled so good. He licked his parched lips and his tongue stuck to them. He stared longingly at the canteens and waited with all the patience he could summon until the soldiers began to eat. Then he edged forward, holding his breath.

He reached a canteen and hefted it to be sure it was a full one. Then he crawled to a row of saddle-bags, took the first set he could reach, and backed away from the camp on his belly.

After the sentry passed again, he was ready to run toward his mule. But suddenly he felt something heavy on his leg, at the ankle.

A large moccasined foot had pinned his leg to the ground.

Chapter Three

"Just hold still, boy, and you won't get hurt."

Roberto started up into the face of an Indian dressed in buckskin pants and a cavalryman's shirt —an army scout. His heart pounded furiously as he tried to decide what he should do.

If this were a white soldier, he thought, *I would spring away suddenly and run for it. But this is an Indian, and he will be ready for any such trick. . . .*

"*Hein ein man-su-ite?*" Roberto said.

That was Comanche for "What do you want?" He knew the scout would recognize it as Indian speech, whether he understood the words or not.

The scout pressed harder on Roberto's ankle.

"Don't try to fool me, boy. You are not a Tejas. You are a part-brown white-boy."

Roberto knew then that the scout was a Comanche, for the word *Tejas* meant *Eaters,* and that was what the Comanche Indians called themselves —Eaters. The five principal Comanche clans were the Buffalo Eaters, the Dog Eaters, the Antelope Eaters, the Fish Eaters, and the Sugar Eaters. And they called all Mexicans brown white-men, just as they called Negroes black white-men and Orientals yellow white-men.

Roberto had lived among various Comanche clans during much of his life. His father had once captured mustangs with Chief Leaning Rock, and they had been good friends. Roberto knew how deeply old Leaning Rock resented any Indians who lowered themselves to become scouts for the U.S. Cavalry.

"You can speak to me in the white man's language, boy," the Indian said. "Why are you trying to steal from the United States Cavalry?"

Roberto did not answer.

The scout frowned down at him and said, "Get up, now, and march ahead of me to the lieutenant. Take the canteen and the saddlebags with you." He stepped back, releasing Roberto's ankle.

Roberto knew he could not get away from this Indian unless he had a chance for a good head start. He decided to obey the command. He would try to explain his predicament and ask the lieutenant for help in getting water and food to his grandfather.

He rose and walked toward the middle of the camp.

The scout behind him said, "Lieutenant, sir, I have caught this part-brown white-boy thief. I have been watching him for half an hour. He came on a mule, which is now hobbled nearby in the grass. He crawled as sly as a fox into our camp. He looks like a wild boy to me. I now turn him over to you, sir."

By this time all the soldiers were watching. The lieutenant, who was a young, lean man with whiskers and black sideburns, came to Roberto and looked at him for a long time before he spoke.

"Now, I wonder," he said at last, "where a boy like you came from. And why he would try to steal from the U.S. Army. If you are in trouble, all you have to do is ask a soldier for help."

"I need your help!" Roberto said quickly.

"Why were you trying to steal?"

"I'm . . . thirsty. I—" Roberto's words suddenly stopped, for he could not speak. His throat was so dry that it seemed to clog and stick. He felt dizzy, and fought to clear his mind.

"You'd better sit down and tell me what this is all about," said the lieutenant. "Thieving government property is a very serious crime. Here, take some water."

Roberto drank from the canteen, letting the wonderful water trickle down his chin and neck. The lieutenant took it away from him presently and said, "That's enough for now. What's your name?"

"Roberto."

"Where did you come from?"

Roberto told him. The lieutenant thought for a long while, then said exactly what Roberto had feared he would say.

"I'll give you a blanket to sleep on tonight. We will start looking for your grandfather at daybreak, and find out if your story is true. It would be impossible to retrace your steps on the prairie at night."

"The moon is bright!" Roberto cried. "It is rising now. I could find—"

"No," said the lieutenant. His voice was firm. "I will give you something to eat, and you must sleep until daybreak."

Roberto knew that he could not convince the lieutenant. He fell silent and stared around the campsite. He noticed that the Indian scout watched him closely and decided to pretend sleep as the lieutenant had suggested. He ate two cold biscuits and a piece of smoked meat that were offered him, then lay on a blanket and closed his eyes, waiting for the camp to become quiet.

Chapter Four

THE fires slowly died. Solders began to snore in
their bedrolls. The horses ceased stamping in the
grass where they had been grazing near the campsite. Somewhere a wildcat screamed, and far off
another answered. The moon rose brightly in the
cooling air, making an endless blue-black wonder of
the sky.

Roberto was motionless on his blanket, between
the lieutenant and the Indian scout, listening to
every sound. Beyond the bedded-down horses he
could hear the sentry riding quietly in the grass. He
would not make his move until the sentry was on
the opposite side of the camp.

He strained to hear the Indian's breathing, to determine whether the scout was asleep; but he could not be sure. He was certain, however, from his knowledge of Indians, that the scout would never sleep deeply when on patrol: an Indian scout always considered himself on duty, even though sentries were responsible for guarding the camp.

Roberto knew that his only chance was to take the Indian by surprise, which would not be easy. He waited a few more minutes, to let everything drowse in the quiet night.

Then he sprang from his blanket. There was no need to be quiet now!

He grabbed a canteen and a set of saddlebags and ran shouting toward the sleeping horses.

"*Yieeee!*" he cried. "Wake up, run, run!"

The horses snorted and whinnied, frightened by the sudden disturbance. Soldiers came out of their bedrolls and the startled camp burst into life.

Roberto leaped onto the back of the horse nearest him. Because there was no bridle, he guided the horse Indian style by its mane. He dug his heels into the animal's flanks. At the forward surge, he draped the saddlebags over its shoulders and slung the water canteen over his own—and headed southwest over the prairie.

"I will find you later, Plato!" he shouted to his mule, listening as the soldiers tried to round up their stampeded mounts. He knew that he would be out of their reach before they could form a pursuit squad; which meant, of course, that they would probably not try to find him until morning. The Indian scout could easily track him then.

But long before they could find him, he thought grimly, he would have provided his grandfather with food and water. He only hoped he was not too late. . . .

He rode through the moon-brightened night. He looked toward the southern horizon for guidance from the mountains, but the distance was too great; despite the moon's brightness, the mountains could not be seen.

He rode on, frantically comparing his present speed on the cavalry mount with his speed during the afternoon on his mule. And he began to realize, although he did not want to admit it, that he could not possibly locate his grandfather before daylight.

By carefully following a course taken from the position of the moon, however, he could ride until he was close, and then find his grandfather in the first light of daybreak.

At last, fearful that he might overshoot his destination, he stopped to rest the horse and wait for dawn.

He sat on the horse until morning. He had no rope with which to hobble it, and he did not dare chance falling asleep and letting the animal wander away. His sense of direction would be keener if he did not sleep, anyway.

As brightness finally streaked across the eastern sky, milky-blue at first, then purple and pink, he scanned the southern horizon for sight of the mountains. Gradually they came into view, hazy ridges growing steadily clearer. He knew by relating his position to them that he had guessed well during the night.

He stood up on the horse's withers, methodically searching the sea of desert grass in every direction. And his heart leaped when finally he saw the splotch of brightness that he knew was the blanket he had staked to the ground beside his grandfather.

Chapter Five

Roberto gave his grandfather only a little water at first. He knew that a person suffering from thirst could be sent into spasms by too much water at once. He bathed the old man's whiskered face and spoke words of encouragement to him.

"You will be all right . . . you will be all right."

When his grandfather revived, Roberto gave him a cold biscuit from the saddlebags to munch on.

"Roberto . . . how did you find your way?"

"By the moon and the stars. You taught me."

His grandfather's face showed gratitude and admiration, but he could not say anything more for a while.

The sun was high when the soldiers, led by the scout on an Indian pony, finally found him. The lieutenant held up his hand for the platoon to halt, then dismounted and knelt over the old man, testing his pulse.

"You were right, lad—it was important to get water to him. I did not believe your story, but now I will forgive you for scattering our horses. It is amazing that you could find your way across the prairie at night."

Roberto remained silent. He glanced at the scout whose face was impassive but whose eyes sent a warm greeting. *You would be a pretty good scout yourself,* the brown eyes seemed to be saying.

"How do you feel, old timer?" the lieutenant asked.

Roberto watched his grandfather's lips move. "More water, please," he said.

The lieutenant reached for the canteen and gave the old man another drink. Then he turned to Roberto. "I am Lieutenant Greentree, First Platoon, Company B, Eleventh Cavalry. We will take care of your grandfather. What is the rest of your name, Roberto? You have a last name, haven't you?"

"Roberto de Alverez Jones," said the boy. "My grandfather is Señor Modesto de Alverez."

"So, you are with your grandfather. Where is your father, Roberto?"

"My father is dead."

The lieutenant cleared his throat suddenly and said, "This sun is much too hot for a sick man. Here . . . I have an idea. We passed a mesquite thicket about two miles back. Private Carlson."

"Sir."

"Ride back and cut some long sticks to make a temporary blanket canopy to protect him. Sergeant Baker."

"Sir."

"Select a man to go with you and ride to Fort Mystic as fast as you can. Report to Colonel Waycross that in my opinion Captain Gregg should be dispatched here with supplies for treating a man suffering from dehydration, malnutrition, and sunstroke. With the colonel's permission, I will expect you back by nightfall. We will camp here tonight."

"Yes, sir," said the sergeant. Saluting, he chose his man and they rode away in a burst of desert dust.

The lieutenant turned to Roberto and said, "Captain Gregg is our garrison doctor. I'm sure the colonel will send him if they have not been having Indian trouble."

"Comanche trouble, sir?" Roberto asked.

"Yes, the Buffalo Eaters," replied the lieutenant.

"The Buffalo Eaters have not been near Fort Mystic lately," said Roberto. "They are in the Glass Mountains below the Pecos River."

"How do you know that?" the lieutenant asked.

"Chief Leaning Rock and my father were friends. I saw him only a few days ago, and he told my grandfather where he was going."

The whole truth was that Roberto and his grandfather had found the old chief badly wounded from a raid on his band by the Kiowas. The Kiowas and the Comanches were traditional enemies. Roberto thought they fought each other more bitterly than ever, since so much of their hunting land had been taken over by the white men. They were frustrated and very angry, and almost anything could set them to fighting. He was not yet sure whether he wanted to reveal to the lieutenant that Chief Leaning Rock had been wounded.

"Lieutenant," said the scout, eying Roberto narrowly, "this part-brown white-boy may know a lot. I do not believe Leaning Rock would tell anybody where he was going unless he had a good reason."

"Do you know him that well?" Roberto asked quickly. "Are you from the Buffalo Eaters?"

The scout threw out his chest and said, "I am Corporal Red Moon, Scout for First Platoon, Company B, Eleventh U.S. Cavalry."

"Oh," said Roberto, "I have heard of you, Corporal Red Moon. You are from the Sugar Eaters—"

"How come you know so much about Comanches? You are just a part-brown young white-boy."

"I . . . think my grandfather needs more water," Roberto said to change the subject.

He knew that the Sugar Eaters had originally been captive slaves in the old Spanish missions. Their name had derived from the contempt of all other Comanches who accused them of doing the white men's work and eating sugar all day. When finally they were freed from slavery, the other Comanche clans would have little to do with them because they had adopted so many of the white man's ways.

Roberto had indeed heard of Corporal Red Moon. Old Chief Leaning Rock of the Buffalo Eaters had told his grandfather last spring: "Red Moon helps the horse-soldiers chase us when we are trying to keep the white men from killing our buffalo. If the white people would stay on their own lands, they would not need protection. Someday I will kill Corporal Red Moon. His ancestors were in slavery to the white man, and yet he helps them against his own people."

Roberto watched Lieutenant Greentree give his

grandfather another drink of water. Then the lieutenant said, "Roberto, I believe your story. If I can be sure that the principal bands of Buffalo Eaters are not on the warpath, I will take my platoon back to Fort Mystic. Will you tell me exactly what you know about them?"

Roberto decided to tell the truth about old Leaning Rock's injury. All the Comanches would be content for a while if the soldiers stayed at the fort. Roberto knew that the sight of roving troops sometimes made young Comanche braves so angry that they would attempt a massacre without waiting for authority from their chiefs. This seemed a chance to create a few weeks of peace, so he decided to take it.

"The Buffalo Eaters are far below the Pecos River," he said. "They were recently raided by the Kiowas who stole some of their women."

"That means," said Corporal Red Moon quickly, "that they will soon return to make war on the Kiowas."

"Not soon," Roberto told them. "Chief Leaning Rock was wounded. They will do nothing until he has recovered. You can be sure of that."

The lieutenant scratched his beard. "Roberto, you seem to like the Comanches very much. Yet they are the most savage tribe in Texas. I don't really understand it."

"They are my friends, Lieutenant! They only want to keep their lands—their buffalo ranges. White men are killing off all the herds of buffalo, and are taking their lands, year after year."

"Say, Lieutenant!" said Corporal Red Moon suddenly. "Now I know who this part-brown white-boy is. He is the wild boy son of famous Mustang Jones who married the Señorita Rosa de Alverez from Chihuahua, Mexico. She was a woman mustang-catcher herself before she died in the smallpox epidemic. This sick, old brown white-man is her daddy and this part-brown Jones white-boy has lived on the desert and in the Mexican mountains all his life. He has never even been to school. He has just run wild!"

The lieutenant took a long and thoughtful look at Roberto. "So . . . that's who you are. Your father was killed trying to catch a big white stallion the mustangers used to call Diablo Blanco. Where have you and your grandfather been?"

"Looking for gold in New Mexico," Roberto said. "We did not find any."

"Haven't you any other relatives you could live with?"

"I can live with the Buffalo Eaters if I want to," Roberto said, trying to control his anger.

White men always wanted him to give up the

31

desert and go live among a lot of people somewhere. That was always the first thing they thought of when he came into contact with them.

The lieutenant said, "I know a horse-buyer who would pay a thousand dollars for that Diablo Blanco stallion your father was after—"

Suddenly Roberto's grandfather raised himself unsteadily to an elbow and shouted in a raspy voice, "No! Do not tempt this boy!"

"Grandfather, lie down!" Roberto said. "We will not go chasing mustangs again," he added quietly. "Don't worry."

Chapter Six

CAPTAIN Gregg, the garrison doctor from Fort Mystic, arrived late in the afternoon. Roberto and his grandfather were taken to the fort the next day and made comfortable in some unoccupied officers' quarters alongside the parade ground. The quarters, constructed of thick adobe blocks, were blessedly cool. But they crawled with scorpions and had to be cleaned out carefully.

Roberto's grandfather recovered in a few days. While waiting, Roberto enjoyed watching the squads drill on the parade ground. Each time the trumpeter blew Officers' Call or Assembly, a thrill raced through him. The idea surged excitedly in his mind that he could become an army scout some day if he wanted to . . . if he ever decided to join the white man against the Indians.

Corporal Red Moon seemed always to be watching him with curiosity. One afternoon, near the garrison blacksmith shop, Roberto asked the scout why he had deserted his own people.

"Deserted?" An expression of pain floated down over Corporal Red Moon's dark face. His eyes were fierce. "Me no desert! Indians must learn that white man will give them education if they stop bloody fighting all the time."

"But they don't need education," Roberto protested. "They just need to be left alone on their buffalo ranges where they have always lived. That's all they ask!"

"No, no," said Red Moon. "You are wrong. Primitive men hold civilization back. Indians die of diseases that tribal medicine man cannot cure just by rattling over the sick people his bag of owls' heads and puma teeth and magic stones. They need white man's medical knowledge, you know that! You wanted Captain Gregg to treat your grandfather, didn't you? You would not have taken him to the Buffalo Eaters' medicine man, would you?"

"No, I would not," Roberto admitted.

"You say Comanches are your friends. Then why don't you help U.S. Army try to civilize them, as I am doing, so they will live better?"

"But the white men will take their lands," Roberto cried.

"Not all of them," said Red Moon. "Maybe . . . I hope."

"That's a very big 'maybe,'" Roberto told him. "The buffalo herds are almost gone now."

"White man is not perfect," said Red Moon. "But neither is Indian. I will tell you this, my part-brown young white-boy friend. Indian warfare must stop, and the U.S. Army will stop it."

"Yes, I know. The army is going to stop the bloodshed if it has to kill every Indian in the land," Roberto said bitterly, and then he said no more. The entire subject confused him.

When he was among the Comanches, he loved them. Their lives were daring and they were very brave. They were honest with each other and they were always good to him. Yet . . . it was true that their medicine men could not cure anything. *Even my own mother,* Roberto thought, *might be alive today if a real doctor had treated her instead of a Comanche medicine man my father brought in as a last hope. . . .*

Fully supplied once more, healthy and grateful to

the cavalry, Roberto set out with his grandfather and the two mules at daybreak of the sixth day. Their destination was a ranch near Fort Worth, where a relative he had never seen—a nephew of his grandfather's—was going to let them live. Roberto had sent word that he would work as a ranch hand to pay for their keep. He did not really want to go there, but his grandfather had said they had no choice, now that the search for gold had failed.

They pushed slowly across the prairie and through a vast desert area in silence. The sun rose higher, scorching the tough buffalo grass, the ironwood and creosote brush, the cactus and mesquite. They crossed an enormous prairie dog town where excitable, chattering rodents lived with rattlesnakes, owls, and scorpions in underground burrows beneath their entrance mounds.

Roberto's mind was now constantly occupied with thoughts of the money that could be made by catching wild mustangs. As if sensing what he was thinking, his grandfather said, "We are *not* going to go after that Diablo Blanco mustang. Put it out of your mind."

Roberto remained silent and the mules trudged on. Once he stopped to kill a huge tarantula with a greasewood stick; again his grandfather stopped to watch a rattlesnake slither into a prairie dog hole.

Finally the old man spoke. His voice suggested that he had been arguing with himself.

"I am too old to chase mustangs, Roberto! And you are too young."

"You have said that many times, Grandfather. I told you not to worry."

"But I know what you are thinking. You have only one thought, and that is Diablo Blanco and the thousand dollars Lieutenant Greentree told you about."

"Grandfather, a person cannot possibly know what is in another person's mind."

"One does not have to be a wizard to read a young boy's mind at a time like this!" his grandfather said.

That evening they reached the eastern edge of the high plains escarpments and led the mules down a rocky path to a sandstone ledge where they decided to spend the night. Fierce heat lightning in the late sky had suddenly brought a threatening darkness. No sooner had they built a fire and cooked their supper than rain came down in blistering sheets. Brilliant bursts of lightning blinded them and thunder shook the earth.

Roberto and his grandfather huddled under an outcropping ledge and his grandfather said, "Do you think we *could* catch mustangs, Roberto? Just you and I?"

"Yes, I do," Roberto said.

"We have only mules. . . ."

"We could find a good water hole and make a snare and catch one mustang. I could gentle him, and then we could ride him to chase down others. We could rope them. We would not have to search for Diablo Blanco unless we wanted to. Any good mustang is worth money if he is properly gentled."

"I thought you wanted to work as a ranch hand. You told me you did."

"If we go there to live, I will want to work and earn my keep. But I would rather catch wild horses."

"Even if we have to live outside all winter?"

"We could find a dugout somewhere on the Pecos . . . near a wild horse range. Or we could dig one."

"There's one thing you would have to promise me, Roberto."

"Yes, Grandfather?"

"You are too young to make the leap. Your father was killed that way, and you must not try it."

"Even when I am older?"

"When you are older, it will be different. But for now you must listen to me."

"I promise, Grandfather," Roberto said quietly.

They sat on the high sandstone ledge, watching the storm pour out of the sky. Brown and white and yellow desert sands, illuminated now and then by lightning chains, swirled and washed in gullies down the ledges toward the desert floor. By late tomorrow the desert might be choked with storms of dust; the next rainstorm might be a year away, but now the desert was a river.

"Roberto, I will tell you something. I do not want to go to Fort Worth, either," the old man said at last. Roberto grinned; a flash of lightning momentarily lit their faces and he thought his grandfather was grinning, too.

Roberto sat on the ledge, enjoying the storm. For a few weeks the desert would turn green with grasses and weeds that lay for months each year in wait of rain. They would shoot up wildly now, and bloom— then quickly die, and the desert would be suddenly brown again.

He would watch it happen, a miracle before his eyes, even as he searched the horizon for signs of mustangs, and the skies for signs of winter.

I promise, Grandfather, he silently said again, *that I will not try to make the leap until I am older. But some day, if I have to, I will make the leap to catch Diablo Blanco.*

Then he smiled at himself in the darkness. It was perfectly all right to dream, he thought, but he should do it while he was asleep!

Chapter Seven

THEY changed their course and went south for several days, camping at night along small, fish-filled streams. They crossed a mountain range and drifted gradually westward again. They reached a rolling wild horse prairie that was surrounded on three sides by jagged mountains and sharp, sweeping desert hills. Puma and antelope were on the prairie, and wolves, coyote, and deer. But, more importantly, herds of mustangs streamed before them, snorting, tossing their wild-eyed heads, and shaking the very earth with their pounding hoofs.

The horses were every hue horseflesh can be—white, dun, sorrel, roan, spotted orange and gray, chestnut, platinum, dappled black and brown. They were descended, of course, from tame horses brought to the New World by Spanish explorers four hundred years earlier. Many of the tame horses had been scattered during Indian raids—eventually to run completely wild and procreate a breed called "mustang." It came from the Spanish word *mesteño*, meaning homeless or stray.

Millions of mustangs now ranged over the wild horse prairies in large herds and small. Each herd was led by a wise old mare, but it was controlled by a restless stallion. His shaggy mane and tail flowed out like flags when, spooked by the approach of anything he had reason to fear, he snorted, reared, wheeled, and thundered away. The herd of mares, and the younger stallions, always instantly obeyed and took flight with him.

"Do you remember the wild horse watering hole," the old man said, "toward the far edge of this prairie?"

"Yes, I remember it," Roberto told him. "There is a mile of scrub oak on the hill behind it. I can see the thicket from here."

"And there is a large live oak tree near the hole, isn't there?"

"Yes, we can rope a mustang from it if we are lucky. I will climb the tree, Grandfather, and wait with a loop," Roberto said.

"And I will lie in the tall grass in a gully beside the hole. I will be able to see you from there. If you can drop a loop over a horse's neck, I will come and rope his legs. Together we can throw him, the way your father always did."

They continued making their plan as they approached the water hole near the scrub oak thicket.

Because of the moisture around the water hole, the bluestem grass was almost shoulder high. Roberto let the mules drink as much as they wanted, then led them into the grass and picketed them where they could graze out of sight.

"Let's hope the breeze is out of the east, Roberto," the old man said, his voice now high with excitement. "Those mustangs may not come close if they smell us here."

Roberto moistened his fingers and held them up to test the wind. "It is from the southeast," he said. "That is good enough."

He tied one end of his best rope around the trunk of the live oak, then climbed the tree and stationed himself out on a large limb. Carefully, he prepared a loop on the other end. Below, near the water hole, his grandfather crawled with his own rope into the tall grass. When he had positioned himself comfortably for a long wait, he called to Roberto in the tree.

"We must be silent now," he said.

"Yes," Roberto answered. "The mustangs might not come until dusk. . . ."

But the herd came late in the afternoon, directly out of the east. Roberto felt the vibrations of the earth even before he saw the horses. They trotted for a while behind the lead mare, who was plainly headed for water with no other thought in mind. Then they were halted by a big dappled stallion which suddenly galloped in a circle around them. He cut them off from the water path for apparently no reason except to demonstrate who was boss. There were thirty or more in the herd.

Roberto glanced at his grandfather who was pointing to the north, then to his ear, indicating that he could hear something in that direction. Roberto looked. To his amazement, another herd was approaching the water hole, charging fast.

Staring at the second herd, Roberto's eyes became glued to the stallion who circled it. This stallion was solid white with a great head that thrust up and backward as he pranced. The muscles of his huge chest rippled like steel springs in the late sunshine. His mane flowed out into a washing splash of dazzling white light, three or four feet long. From his actions, one could plainly see that he was quite aware of the other herd approaching the hole. Suddenly he broke toward the water as fast as he could run, his hoofs beating the prairie to dust as his herd came thundering after him.

Watching, Roberto knew that this was the horse his father had died trying to catch. It was the famed Diablo Blanco, worth a thousand dollars!

He knew, too, that a race was on. Taking up Diablo's challenge, the dappled stallion leading the other herd from the east now broke into a thundering gallop. The herds neared the water hole quickly. When they were no more than two hundred yards beyond the live oak tree where Roberto crouched, the two stallions wheeled suddenly toward each other. They snorted and screamed. They raised their heads high and their teeth glistened as they snarled angry warnings. When they reached each other they were both walking on hind legs, their hoofs slashing like sharpened sledge hammers as they met.

They ripped each other's hides. They tore at ears

and jugular veins, and blood flowed crimson. Shrieks of pain rent the air.

With tails straight out and ears laid back against their heads, the stallions pawed each other until at last, with a mighty lunge, the great white Diablo knocked the dapple off his feet. Then he turned around instantly. As the dapple got up, the white stallion's flying heels shot out with a crash that caved in the dapple's rib cage. The suffering horse bellowed and staggered—with the killer Diablo over him in a flash, pawing him to death.

Roberto was filled with a mixture of hatred and admiration. Diablo Blanco was strong and brave, but he was fantastically cruel. Now he circled not only his own mares but those of the dead stallion too. For half an hour he refused to let any of them get to the water, but circled relentlessly, showing them who was master. To prove his point doubly, he cut out half a dozen younger stallions, one at a time, and chased them away.

Then, as if to tell his mares that they could drink as soon as he was through, Diablo Blanco snorted, bobbed his bloody head and came toward the water hole. He paused directly below Roberto's limb, sensing that something was wrong.

It seemed to Roberto, from this close range, that

the blood was all from the other horse—that Diablo Blanco was scarcely scratched! Poised with his rope, he glanced at his grandfather, silently asking permission to drop the loop. His grandfather nodded quickly.

Holding his breath, Roberto took deliberate aim. He shot the loop downward, watching it settle around the big stallion's neck, then gave it a quick tug to draw it tight.

"You've got him!" his grandfather yelled. "He won't have much fight left in him, Roberto! Turn the rope loose, quickly!"

Diablo shrieked and rose to his hind legs, pawing up at the rope. Roberto turned it loose, for it was tied to the tree trunk. When the rope slackened, the stallion turned to run. But the rope was only thirty feet long.

Diablo Blanco lunged against it and turned himself head over heels in the grass. He bellowed and scrambled to his legs again, spinning round once more to paw at the hideous rope.

"Be careful, Grandfather!" Roberto cried as the old man approached with the other rope, prepared to lasso the stallion's front feet and bring him down.

From his crouch on the tree limb Roberto watched. His grandfather ran closer to the stallion, swinging the loop. The crazed horse reared against the rope that held him fastened to the tree. The old man flung his loop at the horse's front legs. But as it settled over the legs, the first rope suddenly broke, four feet below the horse's neck, setting him free.

"Grandfather!" Roberto cried. All he could do was watch as the frenzied stallion charged his grandfather, pawing him into the earth just as he had pawed the dappled stallion half an hour before.

Chapter Eight

Stunned by the death of his grandfather, Roberto moved for several days as though in a strange, unpitying dream. Loneliness engulfed him, tearing at his heart with the cruel fingers of sudden grief. It seemed, in a dream, that he had crouched on the live oak limb and watched the maddened stallion toss his great head, fling his flowing bloody mane, then wallow contentedly in the water hole for a few minutes, cleaning himself before letting his vast herd of mares come near enough to drink. Then, perhaps with the sound of a sob from Roberto, the horse had wheeled, snorted wildly, and thundered across the prairie whence he had come—with his enlarged herd in frantically obedient pursuit.

In a dream, also, Roberto seemed to have placed his grandfather's lifeless form on one of the mules. He had ridden the other mule himself, leading the way to the top of a high bluff in the mountains where he had buried his grandfather, Indian style, in a mound of stones.

The dream, of course, was hideously true. Slowly, as the days passed and he wandered eastward across the edge of the mountains, he began to accept the appalling reality of being completely alone. But the prairie below, stretching toward the northern horizon in endless undulations of grass, seemed friendly and beckoning. It seemed to say, "You belong here, Roberto—not with your grandfather's nephew who hardly even knows your name. You are smarter than any animal on the desert, you can live here. . . ."

One morning he awakened just as day was breaking. His mind was clear at last. He knew, the instant he thought of it, exactly what he was going to do. He would kill the white stallion!

He took his grandfather's rifle from the pack holster strapped to Socrates—he was using Socrates as a pack animal now. The rifle had not been fired for several days. He removed the cartridges, examined the gun and oiled it with a cleaning kit that was still in his grandfather's gear. He reloaded and tied the holster to Plato so that it would be near him at all times. He broke camp immediately and headed toward the wild horse prairie, where he would begin to search for the killer stallion.

One thing, and one thing only, consumed his mind —and that was the joyful image of the moment he would get Diablo Blanco within the sights of his grandfather's gun with his finger on the trigger.

For three days he waited near the water hole, but Diablo's herd did not come. He crossed the prairie to the north and searched along a creek and finally down a winding river. He combed the edges of a vast canebrake and pushed through dense brush thickets near the hills. Herds of mustangs by the dozen streamed across the prairie before him, but never Diablo Blanco's herd.

He ate rabbit, deer, and quail that he killed along the way. Despite the care with which he apportioned the flour, coffee, and sugar to himself, he soon ran perilously low of everything except the game he was able to kill. He considered going to a trading post on the lower Guadalupe River to trade his extra mule for enough supplies to continue his search. But on further reflection he changed his mind. The so-called civilized white men would undoubtedly try to turn him over to some sheriff to be sent to the ranch near Fort Worth. He headed instead toward the upper

Guadalupe, beyond which he hoped to find a Coman-che band with whom he could trade.

He swam the Guadalupe with his mules at an old buffalo crossing and wound among the moss-draped cypresses in the river canyon until he came to a trail that led back up to the prairie shelf below the mountains. He came out suddenly into the open, and, looking back, stood face to face across the narrow canyon from Diablo Blanco!

The huge horse was "reading" the breeze with his nose high in the air, his nostrils dilating sensitively. His long white mane rippled in the winds blowing in from the Gulf. His tail stood up at a forty-five degree angle, and his ears were forward in an attitude of total alert.

Roberto slipped the rifle out of the pack holster. Quickly he raised it and aimed across at the dazzling white Diablo who, for whatever reason, had run to the edge of the Guadalupe canyon and stopped on its rim.

Staring down the rifle barrel, Roberto beheld the most magnificent wild creature he had ever seen. And he could not pull the trigger. He had come hundreds of miles and had searched for weeks to achieve this moment, but now that the time had come, he could not kill such a beautiful animal.

A sudden new resolution flashed into his mind. He would capture Diablo Blanco! He did not know how, but he would tame this killer horse yet, and then sell him to the horse dealer for enough money to outfit himself for going into the mustang business in a big way.

Can such a thing ever be possible, Roberto asked himself, *when I have only two mules to ride?*

Yes . . . I will go into the mountains and find Chief Leaning Rock, he will help me. . . .

Roberto knew now that there was much about wild horses he must learn. The Comanches were the finest horsemen in America, and many of their best horses were mustangs that had once run wild.

Chapter Nine

H<small>E</small> journeyed southwest until he reached a plateau from which he had a good view of the mountain horizons. There he camped to wait and watch. It would be extremely difficult to locate his Comanche friends without a clue. Comanches who did not know him would most certainly refuse the request he planned to make.

Chief Leaning Rock, if he were still in these mountains, would be in touch with other Comanche bands by smoke signals during the day or fire signals at night. Roberto knew that Chief Leaning Rock had once sent a smoke signal message all the way from Mexico below the Texas border to a Shoshone chief up in Wyoming. It had been relayed by friendly Wichitas, Cheyennes, and various other Shoshone clans.

On the third day of his vigil, he saw smoke puffs rise into the sky at last. He could not be sure they were Chief Leaning Rock's, but they were in the direction the Comanche chief had said he was going for his recovery after the wound by raiding Kiowas.

The mountain up which Roberto rode was rough and steep—the habitat of javalina, mountain lion, and bear. He found a trail at last and on the second day he was stopped by the sudden appearance of a lookout from an Indian encampment.

"I am searching for Chief Leaning Rock," Roberto said to the lookout, who seemed surprised to hear the Comanche tongue. "He told my grandfather he was coming into these mountains to heal his wound."

The lookout was a young brave, tall and muscular, with blood-red skin. He wore only a breech-clout and rawhide-laced moccasins.

"Who are you?"

"I am the boy who helped your chief when he was

crawling with a wounded leg. My grandfather and I were coming out of New Mexico when we found him."

"Where is your grandfather?" the lookout asked suspiciously.

"He is now dead."

The lookout eyed Roberto solemnly. He said, "Tie your mules, leave your rifle in its holster, and follow me on foot, unarmed. I will take you to Chief Leaning Rock. If you are telling the truth I will send someone for your mules and supplies. If you are not telling the truth we will use the top of your head to teach our young boys the art of scalping. . . ."

Roberto followed him up the trail for two miles, then over a series of stone ledges until they came out at last onto a large grassy open mountaintop, completely surrounded by huge volcanic rocks and trees. This, of course, was Leaning Rock's principal winter camp.

"Follow me," the lookout said sharply when Roberto paused to stare around. The grassy area was dotted with tepees made of buffalo hides with openings in the top for smoke to escape. The Indians watched him with narrowed eyes at first, then, as a few of them recognized him, they gathered around and accompanied him to the chief's tepee.

To Roberto's astonishment Chief Leaning Rock looked old and miserable. How long could it have been since they had seen each other—two months at most? The old Indian's arms were thin and his face was gaunt. His smallpox scars, which had seemed a living proof of sturdy vitality when he was in good health, were now a sad and massive disfigurement.

Leaning Rock's clan, and many other Comanches, had been almost wiped out by a smallpox epidemic when he was a child. Vaccination against the malady was prevalent in the white civilization, but Indians and Mexicans did not have the benefit of it yet. Looking at Leaning Rock, Roberto thought of his own mother who had died when she contracted the disease a few years ago in a remote Mexican village far to the south. He remembered her as beautiful—and he would keep that memory.

"I hope you are feeling better," Roberto said.

"My leg is not good," Chief Leaning Rock replied. "It will never be good again." He turned the leg to reveal the scarred muscles of his thigh. It was plain that he would be a semicripple the rest of his life. That meant, of course, that he would no longer be a war chief. He would become a civilian chief and sit in tribal council—but he would never ride in raids again, nor go on horse-stealing expeditions.

A movement in the corner of Chief Leaning Rock's tepee caught Roberto's eye.

"It is the medicine man," the old chief said. "He is going to give me another medicine for my leg."

"Would you like me to leave until he is through?"

"No, you can stay. Perhaps he will make a medicine for your good health, since you are here. Sit down."

Roberto sat beside the ashes in the ring of fire stones at the heart of the tepee. The medicine man, whose back had been turned as he spoke magical messages to his *po-haw-cut,* which was what he called his medicine bag, now turned around. He came toward Chief Leaning Rock, stooped over as he walked, almost danced, jangling the chinaberry beads which hung in a long string around his neck. He was dressed formally, in feathers and bead-decorated buckskins, with eagle feathers braided into his hair.

He reached the chief's injured leg, took it in his hands, and stretched it out straight. Then he reached into his bag and mumbled a magic prayer that Roberto could not understand. Slowly, dramatically, he drew from his *po-haw-cut* a pine cone that was laced with the full length of a six-lined lizard's tail.

"This is my very strongest medicine," he said, and

it was clear that he hoped desperately to improve the condition of his ailing chief.

He placed the medicine on the scarred thigh muscle, leaned over and blew his breath on it, slowly rattled his chinaberry seed beads in the air above it, then mumbled his magical prayer again. At last he picked it up and put it back into his *po-haw-cut*.

"Now," said Chief Leaning Rock, "I would like for you to make a medicine for my young friend. He helped his grandfather save my life one time."

Nodding, the withered old medicine man reached again into his *po-haw-cut* and withdrew a tiny piece of dried meat, the size of a small coin. He reached over and stuck it inside Roberto's ear, then rattled his chinaberry seeds.

"It is a piece of the heart of a white man. If you wear it in your ear, it will keep you safe from the white man's lies."

Roberto solemnly nodded his thanks and waited for the medicine man to leave the tepee.

When he was alone again with Chief Leaning Rock he said, "My grandfather was killed a few weeks ago. I came to ask your help."

"I am sorry to hear about your grandfather," said the chief. "Tell me what happened."

"A wild horse killed him. We were trying to start

into the mustang business together. He had warned me that he was too old and I was too young. He was right."

The chief shook his head sadly. "Your grandfather was my friend. What do you want me to do, Roberto?"

"Send me to Conas with the young braves from your clan."

"That is a special training camp for teaching young men the arts of warfare."

"That is why I want to go."

"Do you want to become a Comanche," the chief asked, "and live with us the rest of your life . . . and fight with us?" His eyes narrowed, for this was the most serious consideration a non-Indian could face.

"No," said Roberto. "I will always be the Comanche's friend, but I will not become one myself."

"Then why do you want to go to Conas?"

"To learn riding and mustang-catching. I was too young to learn enough from my father before he died. I am going to catch Diablo Blanco."

The old war chief shook his head and tried to hide a smile. "Many white men, both black and brown, as well as many red men, have tried to capture Diablo Blanco. Some of them have been killed, including your father."

"I know," Roberto said. He did not dare admit that Diablo Blanco had also killed his grandfather, lest the chief decide against his request. They sat for a while in shadowed silence.

"I must tell you, Roberto," Chief Leaning Rock finally said, "that the war instructor at Conas this year is Yellow Cloud. You have heard of him, I imagine."

"Yes, I have." Roberto shuddered. Yellow Cloud despised all non-Indians with a passion so deep that his reputation had spread far and wide.

"And you still want to go there?"

"Yes," Roberto said. "I am not afraid of Yellow Cloud. I promise you that I will be a good student."

"As long as you know what you are doing, I will send you . . . out of gratitude to your grandfather. But you will have to take the steam baths to cleanse yourself of the stink of your white blood. Yellow Cloud makes all the boys who have white blood take the baths."

"I know," said Roberto with a rueful smile. "I have heard. I want to go."

"And the rest of your life you will be obligated to help the Comanches against their enemies—white white-men as well as brown white-men and black white-men."

Roberto nodded. His pulses pounded at the thought of going to Conas with a hundred Comanche braves. Conas was the principal town of all the Comanche tribes. It was there that they kept their eternal fire burning—*conas* meant "fire" in the Comanche language—and it was there that they conducted their largest and most important training for future warriors.

"I understand," he said. "And I hope you will accept a present that I brought you, Chief Leaning Rock. It is in my pack with my mules."

The old chief looked pleased.

"Your mules will be here soon. The lookout sent for them as soon as he was sure I knew you. What did you bring me, Roberto?"

"A few peyote buttons. They belonged to my grandfather."

"Thank you," the old man said, his eyes misting with appreciation. "They will ease my pain and humiliation. . . ."

Peyote buttons were dried slices from the green heels of the peyote cactus. Anyone who chewed them soon saw wonderful things . . . like fertile pastures where lazy deer and buffalo would walk right up to be killed and slow-flying quail could be caught by hand. Chewing peyote did not make the Indians savage as drinking whiskey did. It gave them the momentary feeling of being in the happy hunting grounds where life was easy and grass was always a very bright apple green.

Chief Leaning Rock, whose heart was weaker than anyone knew, died during the night. No one connected his death with the peyote, for neither Roberto nor the Comanches realized that peyote was a dangerous narcotic.

Chapter Ten

ALL the members of Chief Leaning Rock's clan were grateful that their ailing chief had been treated to the pleasant sensations during his last night on earth. They looked upon Roberto as their special friend and were pleased to have him go to Conas with the young Comanches to learn horsemanship and warfare.

"But that does not mean," said Yellow Cloud the first day of training, "that you can get out of taking the steam baths every week to cleanse yourself."

Yellow Cloud was a broad-shouldered, deep-red warrior whose exploits against the Kiowas, Mexicans, and whites had been spectacular for several years. It was said that he had once traded more than a hundred scalps to a peddler for a pair of boots; he had then tracked down the peddler and killed him for not having warned that boots would not permit the toes to work as well as moccasins did. He had a wide, impassive face and wore a single brilliant eagle feather in his own scalp lock. Anyone who lifted his scalp, he often said, would have himself a twenty-dollar feather.

"I am not trying to get out of the baths," Roberto answered, although he felt secretly embarrassed at being subjected to this rite of purification. He now wore only a breechclout and moccasins, having turned over his clothes and all his belongings, including his mules, to the *adiva*, the woman in charge of the camp. "Is it really true, Yellow Cloud, that you can recognize a white man by his smell?"

"*Yes, puew!*" Yellow Cloud's response was pure disgust. His nostrils flared and his lips curled downward. "White white-men, black white-men, and he-goats all smell alike. We will make a bath for you now. Two more part-white boys have also been sent to camp with us. We will clean all of you if we can."

Roberto and the other two part-white boys were told that they would have to sleep together until they could be rid of their bad smell, which might take all winter. They watched as the fullblooded Comanches prepared their baths.

At the edge of a stony creek, green poles were driven into the ground to form a small framework. Buffalo hides were stretched around its sides. Its top was left open until a fire was built for heating a pile of stones. A blanket was then placed over the top of the bath and a part-white boy was made to crawl inside and dip water over the hot stones with a gourd. The vapors cleansed him.

"Tonight," Yellow Cloud told them when they had finished bathing, "you will chew sassafras roots and spicewood leaves and spit on your blankets. That will help."

That night Roberto talked to his two part-white companions about Yellow Cloud's contemptuous treatment of them.

"He hates white blood so much that only three of us have been sent here this year," said one of the boys. "Did Chief Leaning Rock send you?"

"Yes, he did," said Roberto. "Were both of you sent by chiefs?"

They nodded and one of them said in a low voice, "Roberto you may be in danger from Yellow Cloud.

I have heard that he believes that was poison you gave Chief Leaning Rock."

"I gave him some of my grandfather's peyote," Roberto explained. "He was one of the best friends I ever had!"

"Just the same, you should keep a sharp eye on Yellow Cloud."

"What about you two?"

"We are safe as long as his hatred is chiefly for you."

They lay in silence and Roberto vowed that he would not turn his back on Yellow Cloud for an instant.

The stream near Conas flowed across a level area nestled among some rolling grassy hills above the Colorado River in central Texas. The meadow was dotted with mesquite clumps, small cedar brakes near the hills, and occasional live oak motts—havens for deer and wolves.

The Comanches, Roberto soon realized, spent all their time, when not actually at war, in preparation for war. Yellow Cloud's training encampment taught the boys everything that might be connected with the success or failure of a massacre or a horse-stealing raid.

A herd of trained and semitrained horses were patrolled in a prairie basin to the south of the camp. Hundreds of horses were there. As wild mustangs were captured and gentled in training, their left ears were split to mark them from wild horses, and they were put into the Comanche herd. Every Comanche horse thus had a split ear. A chief's horse had two split ears.

Roberto learned to track through brush and over the desert prairies. He leaned which cacti would provide water and which roots and herbs would keep him alive when no other food was available. He learned the arts of longbow and gun. He learned to stop the flow of blood with pressure pads and rawhide tourniquets. He learned to send smoke and fire signals and to paint messages on buffalo bones and stones for the instruction of other Comanches who might come upon the scene of a massacre or a burned-out camp. He learned the war whoop, which sounded like a loud and very shrill gobble of a wild turkey. He went into the hills and over the prairies and onto the desert for days at a time, learning to track others who had gone ahead of him, or trying to travel without leaving a trail that could be followed.

During the winter he was permitted to wear animal skins. He still slept in a tepee with his two part-white companions, and once each week they went to the creek, built a fire among the stones, and took their cleansing baths. Roberto had worked hard to be a good student, and one of his companions suggested that Yellow Cloud's attitude toward him was beginning to soften. But Roberto did not really think it was, for Yellow Cloud gave him strange sidelong looks and sometimes circled around him at a distance, watching everything he did. On the surface, Yellow Cloud seemed to have become more friendly.

He drew Roberto aside one day to speak privately to him and said, "You do not smell so bad now. I think you could become a Comanche if you wanted to. You are the best student in the camp."

Roberto's pulses pounded, for it was dangerous to say no to Yellow Cloud.

"Thank you very much, but . . . I am going to hunt for a white stallion called Diablo Blanco as soon as our training here is completed. I am going to become a professional mustanger."

Just as Roberto had feared, Yellow Cloud's wide face darkened with anger. His nostrils flared, and his eyes bored into Roberto's.

"Do you think you are better than Indians? Is that why you do not want to be a Comanche?"

"No, I don't—"

"Then why would you rather chase a wild horse than raid Kiowas and massacre white men?"

Roberto knew that he had to give Yellow Cloud some kind of an answer. He decided to tell him the truth—as gently as he could.

"That's exactly what I mean, Yellow Cloud. The Comanches are always at war. I do not see any reason to be at war all the time."

"White man wants our lands, that is why!" Yellow Cloud shouted. The cords and muscles in his neck stood out and the veins at his temples began to swell.

"But the Kiowas and the Wichitas and even the poor Sugar Eaters do not want your lands. Yet you kill them every chance you get."

"They are bad! They steal our horses! They steal our women! They are our enemies!" Yellow Cloud fumed and glared in silence for a few moments and then he said, "When the Kiowas next make a raid on Fort Mystic, we are going to raid them. We will kill all their women and children and their old people and their dogs and horses. We will stampede their buffalo herds across the Palo Duro into our own buffalo ranges." Yellow Cloud angrily pointed his finger at Roberto and shouted, "You could come with us, but you think you are too good to be an Indian."

Roberto let the warrior's temper cool a bit before answering. And then he asked, "Do you know when the Kiowas are going to raid Fort Mystic?"

Yellow Cloud's eyes narrowed into cunning slits. "There are some things you are not allowed to know unless you become a Comanche. If you do not, I hope you are at Fort Mystic with your white-stink friends and Corporal Red Moon when the raid comes!"

Chapter Eleven

For several days Yellow Cloud would say nothing to Roberto. But Roberto knew that the war instructor watched him all the time and gave much thought to what should be done with him. He wondered if his friendship with the departed Chief Leaning Rock would be enough to save him from Yellow Cloud's bitterness. There was no animal on earth as danger-ous as a wounded Comanche warrior; when the warrior's pride was wounded instead of his body, he

71

would be doubly dangerous, for he then had all his physical capacities to implement his savage cunning.

During the shield-and-lance training, Roberto discovered just how much Yellow Cloud disliked him.

The shields were made of dogwood or hickory hoops covered tightly with the tough neck skin from a buffalo and sewed many times with rawhide thongs. The lances were long wooden shafts of ash or Osage orange, tipped with pieces of bone that had been carved and sharpened into oversized arrowheads.

The training included both warfare practice and buffalo killing. Man-to-man combat was conducted with the bone points of the lances covered with strips of horsehide wrapped into hard balls, and the method of teaching was a "game" called *break the lance*. Roberto noticed that Yellow Cloud's mouth drew into a sinister smile as he began the instruction.

"You can be first, my part-brown, white-boy student who does not want to be a Comanche. You have been a very good student and I am sure you will learn the art of the lance very quickly!"

Yellow Cloud was sitting on his pony with his battle-scarred shield on his arm. His eyes narrowed and Roberto knew that the angry warrior was going to treat him roughly during the demonstration.

"Now, get on your horse," said Yellow Cloud, "and ride over to that mesquite clump, then turn around. Carry your shield like this and hold your lance in this position." He demonstrated elaborately. "Ride toward me when I ride toward you. The objective in actual warfare is to run the lance through your opponent's chest or stomach. In practice warfare, we try to break the opponent's lance or knock him off his horse by ramming him with the horsehide ball where it would be a fatal blow. A well-trained warrior can break his opponent's lance and then run him through. Now, everyone watch closely as I demonstrate. . . ."

Riding toward the mesquite clump, Roberto knew that the other boys were watching with great interest. They all suspected that Yellow Cloud intended to be rough on his star pupil, and they did not mind. They resented the fact that the star performer was one who had to take white stink-baths and chew on spicewood leaves.

"Now!" Yellow Cloud cried, kicking his pony's flanks and lowering his body over the pony's neck, his shield up and his lance thrust out. The sunshine glistened on his bare red shoulders, the outlines of which Roberto could just see above the rim of the shield. As he came, he held the lance so straight that the entire length of it was hidden behind the tough horsehide ball.

Staring at the onrushing angry instructor, Roberto felt paralyzed for a moment. Then he leaned over, thrust out his lance, and kicked his own horse into action.

They charged. Almost before they reached each other, it seemed, Roberto heard his lance crack and felt a stinging blow near his wrist. Another blow struck his stomach well below his chest, and he went sprawling from his horse, unable to get his breath.

He lay on the ground for several moments, refusing to let himself writhe in pain. He gasped for breath, but he held himself rigid, for he did not want to clutch at his stomach. He thought he might black out completely from lack of breath, but gradually his vision cleared as the blessed air returned to his suffering lungs.

"Well, well," said Yellow Cloud, "I believe our part-white student got hurt. Get up, now, and watch for a while."

Then Yellow Cloud did something that caused Roberto to hate him. He put the other students to charging against each other, instructing them from his pony, shouting corrections and suggestions for improvement. But when Roberto felt ready to resume, he found himself again matched with Yellow Cloud.

Each time they charged, Yellow Cloud knocked him cruelly off his horse with the rawhide ball, and then strutted around him astride his pony, holding his lance high in the air, while all the boys laughed and jeered. Roberto knew that they had to laugh or insult Yellow Cloud, but it did not make him feel any better when he lay in a dusty heap on the ground.

He was poorly trained in the art of shield-and-lance combat. He knew, by the time it was finished, that any boy in the camp could beat him, and he burned with humiliation, even though he had never wanted to be a warrior in the first place.

Chapter Twelve

At last Yellow Cloud began the part of the training that Roberto had been waiting for. He called together all the boys who were ready for the special horsemanship instruction.

"First you must learn to braid buckskin arm loops into your horse's mane. Your life may depend on the strength of your braids."

As the young men watched intently, Yellow Cloud demonstrated with heavy buckskin thongs the method of braiding loops into the long mane of a training horse. He then placed a rawhide surcingle, with short loops of buffalo sinews for stirrups, over the horse's back and cinched it tight.

"Now you will see how important the braids are,"

the warrior told them. He put a foot into one stirrup and an arm through a loop in the mane, drawing himself instantly off the ground into a hanging position at the horse's side. "Notice that both my hands are free. I can shoot an arrow or a gun or throw a lance without exposing myself at all. I simply must manage to keep my horse between me and the enemy."

Yellow Cloud then showed them how he could drop from a normal position astride the horse to a hanging position merely by throwing one foot over into the stirrup on the opposite side and letting his arm slide through a mane loop. He did it at a trot and then at full gallop.

"Part-brown white-boy, you can try first," he said. His eyes were fierce and cunning slits in his face. Roberto knew that Yellow Cloud wanted him to fail.

But he did not fail. He had probably spent more time on a horse during his life than the Comanche boys had, for they were not allowed horses of their own until they completed training.

He sprang astride the horse, threw his leg over and let himself dangle off the ground at the horse's side. He performed both trotting and at full gallop, just as Yellow Cloud had demonstrated.

"Not too bad for a part-brown white boy!" Yellow

Cloud admitted. Some of the boys started to laugh, but Yellow Cloud shouted angrily at them and their faces quickly sobered.

After several days of practicing, Roberto could shoot an arrow or a firebrand from underneath the horse's neck. He could swing himself from side to side, picking up arrows from the ground on alternate sides of the horse at full gallop. He beat all the other boys in his class at this difficult task. He thought they respected him, even though Yellow Cloud had caused them to dislike him.

And he excelled at the trick of riding on the side of his horse into a mustang herd, to single out the lead stallion, drive him from the herd, and rope him. He learned to throw the mustang, leap down, and tie its forelegs before it could get up. He learned to gentle the wild ones by talking to them blind-folded, rubbing their backs and patting them, quietly placing a surcingle on them, and then riding them, letting them run themselves into exhaustion if they wanted to.

Frequently when he was out in the hills alone he would think about the shield-and-lance training he had virtually missed and he would cut himself a long pole and practice the lance maneuvers he had watched the other boys perform. He would charge toward trees, aiming at certain twigs and leaves. He would ride fast through heavy brush, deftly using his lance to ward off the thorny branches that tore at him. To practice against moving targets he would ride among wild cattle or buffalo herds, thrusting his makeshift lance at a certain horn or at a certain spot on the neck or shoulder.

Yellow Cloud, of course, did not know that Roberto was secretly practicing the lance. And Roberto noticed that Yellow Cloud's scowl became deeper with the perfection of each new phase of his training. He began to wonder whether his war instructor intended to let him go alive if he did not promise eventually to become a Comanche.

Chapter Thirteen

ONE morning after they had finished a difficult session of lariat practice, Yellow Cloud told all the boys to line up in an unusual formation. They placed their ropes in neatly coiled piles and stood beside their horses, listening.

"Today we will have the ring tournament," he told them.

They cheered, for each year this was a special event at the warfare school. Twenty-five posts were stuck into the ground about fifty yards apart to form a large circle on the prairie. Rings were suspended from sticks fastened to the tops of the posts. The contest was to ride a circle around the posts at a full gallop, gathering on the lance as many rings as possible. The record at Conas was twenty—achieved many years before by Yellow Cloud himself.

Roberto had been looking forward to this tournament ever since he had begun to practice secretly with a makeshift lance.

The morning was spent laying out the tournament ground and placing the posts and rings. During the afternoon the contest was to be held.

Yellow Cloud demonstrated for a while. He rode fast around the posts, taking the rings with his lance point. All the boys wondered, for Yellow Cloud was, if anything, better now than when he had established the Conas record.

"Are you afraid to try first?" he asked Roberto. A snarling grin on his face made his teeth glisten in the early sunshine.

"I am not afraid," Roberto said quietly, although he had become very much afraid of Yellow Cloud.

"You have performed fairly well at everything else, but you are no good with the lance," Yellow Cloud said. "Go ahead and ride—we will see how many rings you can take."

Roberto mounted, kicked his horse with his heels, and bent low with his lance as he approached the first post, much as he had so many times in the brush.

The rings were larger than the leaves and twigs he had learned to stick with his makeshift lance, and therefore easier to hit. He rode fast around the circle of posts and returned at the end with twenty-one rings.

Yellow Cloud's nostrils flared as he counted them.

"Nobody has ever done this before," he said. "My record was twenty. You have broken it."

"I have been practicing secretly," Roberto admitted, glancing at the other boys who listened and watched intently. He was sorry he had broken the record, for Yellow Cloud's anger was growing dangerous.

"When have you had time to practice?"

"When I am out chasing mustangs or in the hills, tracking, I always practice."

"Have you decided to take over your own training?"

"No, I—"

"Why do you want to stay in Conas if you think

you know better than I know how to teach you?"

"But don't you see, Yellow Cloud?" Roberto asked urgently. "I have learned something new that could be of value to all the boys. I learned to spear leaves, which are much smaller targets than the rings. That is why the rings were easy for me. If the others practiced on smaller objects—"

"So, you are now the instructor!" Yellow Cloud's face turned hideous with rage. He stamped the ground as he stared at Roberto. "So you have taught yourself how to use the lance . . . well, I will give you a good test!" He grabbed a lance from the boy nearest him and leaped upon his pony. "You and I will play *break the lance,* my stuck-up part-brown white boy. We will not even use our shields!" He dug heels into his pony and galloped out among the ring posts. In a cloud of dust, he wheeled his pony around. It reared high as it turned. Then Yellow Cloud lowered his lance and shouted to Roberto.

"Now we will see how well you taught yourself!"

Again he dug heels into his pony and came charging at Roberto with his lance. There was no ball of horsehide at the end of it this time.

Roberto had no choice. If he sat still, Yellow Cloud would run him through, to make an impressive lesson to all the other boys. He kicked his horse and leaned forward over its neck. He lowered his own lance and charged toward Yellow Cloud, more frightened than he had ever been. He could see Yellow Cloud's bulging strong arm and knew that he would have no chance to deflect the lance without a shield; he was simply not strong enough. As they met, Roberto deftly swung his left leg over into the opposite stirrup and thrust his left arm through the mane loop, dropping alongside his horse just in time for Yellow Cloud's lance to pass above him. He heard the other boys cheer.

Guiding his horse by its mane, he turned around in time to see Yellow Cloud rear and whirl his pony for another thrust.

Once more astride, Roberto dug heels into his horse and went again to meet the attack. He knew his chances were much better than if he stood still. He could see that Yellow Cloud's face was twisted with humiliation for having been tricked in combat by a student.

This time Roberto swung quickly to the opposite side of his horse to escape the lowered lance, and again the boys cheered, making Yellow Cloud even angrier.

Roberto knew that he must do something drastic, for it would be impossible to elude Yellow Cloud's lance much longer. He did not dare kill Yellow Cloud, for all the boys in Conas would then be after him and all Comanches would consider him their enemy. Turning to meet the next thrust, he had an idea.

As Yellow Cloud bore down on him for the third time, he swung himself upside down underneath his horse's belly. Yellow Cloud's lance passed by so close that it cut his horse's hip. But the horse had courage and did not flinch. Roberto knew that his only chance was to act very fast, for Yellow Cloud's rage would now be overwhelming.

Clinging to the mane by one hand, he hit the ground with his feet and bounced astride his wounded horse, even as he wheeled it around. He went toward Yellow Cloud before the maddened warrior had time to turn for another charge. He lowered his lance, rushed at Yellow Cloud quickly, and then did what he had to in order to save his life. First making it clear that he could have run his lance through Yellow Cloud if he had wanted to, for he had the warrior off balance now, he ran it through the pony's neck instead.

The pony stumbled instantly, sending Yellow Cloud into the dust.

Roberto yanked the bloody lance free, wheeled his

horse again, and scooped up as many of the lariats from the ground as he could quickly reach with the point of his lance. Then he headed for the desert hills as fast as he could. Dozens of the boys ran for their horses and came after him, shouting and even practicing the war whoop. But he had a good start, and he knew they would not catch him if his horse did not falter.

The horse seemed only superficially wounded. He galloped all afternoon, and Roberto was deeply grateful to him.

With neither clothes nor supplies, nor even a pack mule, Roberto knew that he must now face the wild horse prairies alone. But he did have three lariats, he realized joyfully when he had a chance to untangle them. The lariats could save him; and the simple act of holding them in his hands gave him a sense of safety. Otherwise he had only the horse, a Comanche lance, a breechclout, and moccasins.

He could no longer hear the pack of boys following, but they would most surely be assigned the task of tracking him down, for their training. To confuse his trail, he rode up the middle of streams—each time he came to one shallow enough—sometimes riding, sometimes carefully leading the horse. Sometimes he crossed a stream and then crossed back a hundred yards or so further on.

Resting his horse at brief intervals, he washed the cut on its hip with cool water which he dipped with one of his moccasins. Fortunately, the cut was not deep. At dusk he looked for a place on the prairie to spend the night. The spring air was chilly when he finally hobbled his horse and lay in a bed of oak leaves at the edge of some low scrubby hills. Naked except for his breechclout, he burrowed under the leaves to keep warm, thinking for a moment of the day he would capture Diablo Blanco. Far away in the hills he could hear wolves howling.

Chapter Fourteen

THE night was black with an overcast sky. Roberto awakened at the sound of wolf howls which now seemed much closer than when he had gone to sleep. He tested the wind with a wet finger. His scent was probably wafting in the direction of the wolves. He lay in the leaves, listening and wondering.

If only he had a fire . . . wolves had never been known to come close to a campfire . . . but such thoughts, he knew, were idle . . . he had no fire.

His horse snorted and stamped restlessly in the grass nearby. He knew that the horse was aware of the wolves.

Suddenly he sprang from the leaves and went to

his horse to unhobble it. Wolves could kill a hobbled horse easily, but they were afraid of animals that were tied to stakes or trees. He remembered his grandfather having explained that wolf hunters often baited traps with live animals staked out on the prairie. Wolves, sly by nature, had now grown wary of anything tied.

Working in the darkness, he tied his horse to a tough scrub oak, giving it plenty of room to protect itself if it should be attacked. Then he burrowed back into his own bed, hoping his human scent would frighten the wolves away from him.

The wolves did come close, howling in a circle around his horse, but they did not attack. At daylight he examined the horse and could see no evidence of the legs having been chewed.

He selected a temporary campsite on a small mesa above a steep slope which dropped off into the prairie. The mesa was high enough to give him a good view of the horizon in three directions. He could quickly escape down the slope if he should be attacked from the scrub oak hills. He knew that, until he had caught a mustang and gentled it for trading, he must work from this camp and not wander aimlessly.

Food now became his only thought. He stalked

and finally killed a young deer with his lance. Late in the afternoon he felt it was safe to build a fire. Certainly, he could not take a chance on smoke during the daytime. With straps from his surcingle he made a firebow and spun a spindle of greasewood until he had a blaze going. With the bone point of the lance, he cut some meat from the deer, but it was very difficult. The point had no real cutting edges. He ate at last, and his firelight died.

He heard no wolves at all, for which he was grateful, for he did not want to lose his supply of fresh meat. The next day he would find a pole and suspend the meat high in the air to keep it out of reach of wolves while he went in search of a mustang. At last he banked his coals to keep them alive and went to sleep.

The next morning he found a mustang herd shortly after sunup. He prepared a coil of rope and slipped down alongside his horse. He circled the mustangs casually for half an hour and then gradually went closer. Staying on the outside of his horse, dangling from the stirrup and rings, he managed to ride among them. Already he had singled out a young stallion, and with a gentle tug on his horse's mane he cut the stallion off from the herd.

He swung his loop quickly. By the time it landed over the stallion's head, the entire herd had spooked and thundered toward the horizon. But he had his quarry.

The young stallion reached the end of the rope in a surge of power. The tame horse, an old hand at roping, drew back at exactly the right time. The stallion tumbled in a heap and Roberto was on top of him, tying his forelegs.

The stallion got up and reared wildly, but he could not run. While the trained horse held him, Roberto circled him on foot, finally swinging another loop that caught the hind legs, once more throwing him to the ground. The young horse struggled on his side, kicking the dirt and screaming desperately. Roberto stood by and let him wear himself out.

After three hours the exhausted horse lay still. Roberto removed his breechclout and tied it over the horse's face for blinders. All the while he talked gently to the terrified animal.

"If you should get away from me," he said in a soft voice, "I would have no clothes except my moccasins. Please be gentle. I will not hurt you. I wonder what name I should give you. You are very tough. I think I will call you Cactus. Please, please do not run away with my one small bit of clothes...."

He picketed his own horse, then placed the surcingle on Cactus, patting him and murmuring gently. With the long rope still tied to his tame horse's neck, he released Cactus's legs at last and let him up. Blindfolded, the horse stood still until Roberto approached, and then despite the blinders he screamed and ran in a circle.

Roberto let him run. Leading his own horse, he moved Cactus to the edge of the hills and tied him to a tree where he could graze and sleep during the night.

For three mornings in a row he had to rope the wild stallion's feet and throw him to the ground, where he lay kicking and snorting until he was exhausted. But each night he grazed at the end of his rope, which was good; for mustangs frequently refused to eat in captivity and were soon dead.

Roberto rode him on the fourth morning.

He had somewhat soothed Cactus's nerves by now. He walked up to him and placed the halter over his head. "Thank you for not biting me," he said. "You see, I am not a bad fellow." He rubbed the horse's back gently and cinched the surcingle tighter. When he decided the time had come, he casually untied the long rope and sprang suddenly onto the wild horse's back. Startled, Cactus reared for a moment, and then shot across the prairie as hard as he could run. Roberto held a slack rein, prepared to stay with him until he ran it out of his system.

They were a good fifteen miles from the camp on the mesa when the horse finally gave in and slowed down to a walk.

"Cactus, I like you," Roberto said to the horse, patting the animal's steaming neck. "I wish I did not have to sell you. But I need a knife very badly. And I will need some clothes, especially boots, when I go after your big white cousin called Diablo Blanco. Someday, somehow, I will capture him, Cactus, and I will be rich. But for now, old boy, we have a long walk back to my camp. You put up a very good fight, I am proud of you. . . ."

Chapter Fifteen

Roberto sold Cactus to a peddler he ran into while on his way to the trading post on the Guadalupe. The peddler was a tall man with black sideburns and a white hat. His wagon contained everything that could be called the "latest" in pots and pans, coal oil lamps, reading spectacles, Bibles, almanacs, and furniture for the frontier. He sat in the high spring seat of his wagon and his gaunt face looked down sadly from underneath the white hat brim.

"Me like 'em horse. Indian boy like 'em nice red beads?" He dangled a string of beads which he drew from a box in his wagon and made gestures indicating that he would trade.

Observing the peddler's appreciative eye each time he looked at the horse, Roberto decided to ask a stiff price. An unbroken mustang was worth about five dollars, a gentled one about twenty-five. But Cactus was an exceptionally fine young stallion. Roberto took a stick and, without uttering a word, marked $35 in the dirt alongside the trail where they had met.

The peddler climbed from his seat and stared at the mark on the ground.

"Thirty-five dollars—that's heap much wampum," he said, and Roberto kept a straight face although he was laughing inwardly. He glanced down at himself, clad only in a badly-frayed Comanche breechclout and moccasins. He was not surprised that anyone not thoroughly familiar with Indians might think he was one. This peddler was probably venturing farther west than he had ever been before.

Roberto pointed with the stick to the mark he had made on the ground, then held out his hand.

The peddler said, "I'll give you twenty, not a cent more. Understand 'em twenty dollar offer?" He took the stick from Roberto and marked $20 in the dirt.

Roberto scowled as angrily as he could, and pointed impatiently at his thirty-five-dollar mark.

"You drive heap good bargain, Hiawatha," the peddler said forlornly.

Still without smiling, Roberto held out his hand.

"I may die in the poorhouse, but I like this horse. All right, here you are."

The peddler took a small roll of bills from his pocket and handed it to Roberto. The roll proved to contain twenty-one dollars. Roberto shook his head again but the peddler quickly said, "All right, all right, it was an honest mistake. At least you know how to count. I don't think you Indians are half as dumb as you act. I'll bet you think I was trying to cheat you." His lean face broke into a trace of a self-conscious grin as he counted out the rest of the money from another pocket. "Well . . . I *was* trying to cheat you, but I didn't get away with it. I'm glad you don't understand English."

Roberto took the money and bowed to the man. He said, with a flourish, "Sir, you will have to supply your own bridle or halter. I have only one. If you should happen to let this animal loose accidentally, he will probably try to find me. We have been very good friends. He was a wild mustang just three weeks ago. His name is Cactus, and I would judge him to be about two years old."

The peddler's eyes popped open wide.

"Well, I'll just be . . . where on earth did you learn to speak English like that?"

"From the Mexicans." Roberto returned the man's grin. "Adios, señor!" he cried, clutching the money. He gave a Comanche war whoop just for fun, leaped upon his horse, and rode away toward the trading post on the Guadalupe.

Chapter Sixteen

He outfitted himself with a secondhand army blanket, matches in a waterproof box, flour, sugar, a skillet with a folding handle like those he and his grandfather had used, canteen, spade, skinning knife, ax, sheepskin pad for a saddle, and a used army rifle. He could not afford a really good hunting rifle, but the used one fired all right. He tried it out on a stump behind the store before he bought it.

His heart and spirits soared as he headed northwest toward the tall-grass water hole on the far side of the prairie where he had first seen Diablo Blanco.

For many weeks he had been working out a plan for capturing the great white stallion. He would need at least two more fast horses . . . as well as luck.

Just as he had captured Cactus, he worked diligently until he captured and gentled two more mustangs. The job required the entire summer, because the addition of the second new horse made it much harder to control both of them.

With his ax, Roberto finally cut post oaks in the hills and dragged them down to the edge of the prairie. There he made a small corral by fencing across the opening to a narrow box canyon. And there he set up his permanent camp, where he would return to continue mustanging after he sold Diablo and had enough money to outfit himself in a real way.

He rode the horses every day until they were exhausted and quite obedient. He braided arm loops into their manes and trained them to carry him full gallop at their sides. The task required all the hours of daylight each day, but he hunted for food as he trained the horses, and all the while he kept an eye out for Diablo's herd.

It did not surprise him that the devil horse was not hard to find when the time came at last to attempt the capture. It was late September now, and the weather had cooled a bit. He dreamed of becoming rich before winter. September was known as the "Comanche Moon," a good time for horse-stealing. Perhaps it would prove a good time for horse-capturing, too . . . .

He got his first glimpse of Diablo on the rim of a river canyon, much like the spot where he had once decided not to pull the trigger when he had the big horse in his gun sights. Diablo reared to all his magnificent height. His long mane flowed out and glowed white against the sky. With his ears back, he snorted angrily, wheeled, and fled the canyon. His herd followed, sending dust clouds high into the sky.

Roberto began the pursuit. He knew that none of his horses could possibly catch Diablo Blanco in a race. His plan was to use them in relays, keeping the white stallion on the move for days until he was exhausted.

Roberto had learned at Conas that wild horses were creatures of stubborn habit. Even though they sometimes roamed for many miles out of curiosity, or ran for hours on end if they were being chased, they always moved in great circles back to the grassland they considered home. By following the dust trails raised by Diablo's herd, Roberto knew that in time he would be back in this part of the prairie.

He kept Diablo moving all day; toward nightfall, when he passed near his camp, he changed to a fresh mount. Then he followed by moonlight. He feared he had lost Diablo before daybreak, for his only clue to direction was the sound of pounding hoofbeats. But the early sunlight showed him dust on the horizon again.

The herd became smaller as the mares and younger stallions fell behind and scattered out alone. During the third day he caught several glimpses of the big white horse.

Diablo was now visibly tired. He would stop on a knoll or at the top of an incline, staring at his pursuer with flared nostrils, breathing heavily. He would paw and stamp the ground the moment Roberto came into sight. And with no more than the briefest hesitation he would be off again for a five- or six-mile run.

Roberto now neared exhaustion himself. That night he hung his arms through the rings and tried to sleep as he rode—but he was not very successful. Just at daybreak he tied his horse to a mesquite tree and dropped into the grass for a few minutes' sleep. He lay with his face toward the east so that the first sunshine would wake him, in an hour at the most. Diablo would not sleep during that hour. The devil horse, he knew, would stand alert on some high place and watch.

On the fourth day he saw the big stallion frequently. Diablo ranged completely alone now. Tomorrow, Roberto decided, would be the day to attempt the catch.

He slept an hour at daybreak again. He had rested his Comanche horse well for his final pursuit. When he passed near his camp on the mesa that morning, he changed to the Comanche horse. He tied three good ropes to his surcingle and set out after Diablo at the most leisurely pace possible.

He soon saw the white killer-devil standing on the rim of an arroyo, glaring back at him pitifully.

"I am sorry to treat you this way, Diablo," he said joyously. "But you are going to be mine today . . . my father died trying to leap onto your back, and you killed my grandfather when a rope broke. I could have shot you last summer but I didn't . . . you are going to make me rich . . . ."

Diablo seemed to wait longer than usual before he broke into a run toward the horizon this time.

Roberto walked the white horse down once more, then dug heels into his Comanche horse, and flew in swift pursuit.

The stallion was taken by surprise, for this had not been the pattern of the past few days. He ran for a mile, then looked back. Roberto was close, urging the Comanche horse on.

Diablo snorted and squealed in a mixture of fright and bitter anger. He thundered ahead, skimming across the undulating prairie for five miles before pausing to look back. Still Roberto was right on him.

Away he went again, but Roberto closed in rapidly, for his horse had plenty of reserve strength. Leaning forward, he let a loop in his lariat and swung it swiftly over his head, urging the Comanche horse as hard as he could.

He threw the lariat and watched it settle around Diablo's neck. His heart pounded furiously—this was the moment he had worked toward for more than a year.

Diablo reached the end of the rope, lunged against it, and tumbled head over heels into the grass.

Roberto leaped down and ran to tie the killer horse's forelegs. But Diablo was too quick, despite his weary condition, and still much too strong. With a wild squeal, he righted himself and nipped Roberto painfully on the leg as he came up. Then he reared, ready to strike at his adversary with his front hoofs.

But the Comanche horse backed away expertly, tightening the rope and veering Diablo's blow to one side.

Diablo snorted and wheeled, then went at the Comanche horse. He walked on his hind legs, pawed and bit, exactly in the manner of his attack on the stallion he had killed the year before at the water hole.

Roberto caught hold of a ring in the mane of his Comanche horse, leaped astride, and quickly untied the rope, setting Diablo free. Then he reined away from the maddened stallion.

"I am going to capture you today, Diablo!" he shouted in anguish. "You are only free for a little while!"

The gigantic horse watched him for an instant of bewilderment. The sight of a horse and rider was apparently more formidable than the sight of either a horse or a man alone. He snorted and squealed wildly, then broke into a furious run toward the horizon.

Roberto immediately dug heels into the Commanche horse and went after him. "I will not let you rest, Diablo!" he shouted.

This time they ran four miles before Diablo slowed up visibly. He still dragged the lariat which had been untied from the other horse, and it seemed to be a distraction—perhaps even a handicap.

Roberto decided not to lasso him again. He took a short length of tie rope, with which he had planned to hobble Diablo's forelegs, and leaned forward as he approached the fast-running stallion. He remembered in a flash that his father had been killed attempting this feat. He remembered, too, that he had promised his grandfather he would not do this; but he had been younger then, and he felt that he had trained himself well enough to satisfy his grandfather if the old man were here to watch . . . .

He drew alongside Diablo and leaned over as far as he could. Then, springing mightily, he leaped onto the killer horse's back. It was the broadest, strongest back he had ever sat astride. The power still churning in those tired muscles, as the maddened animal pounded the prairie, was simply astonishing.

Roberto quickly gathered up the lariat with which he had roped Diablo. He let the horse run as hard as he could for half an hour, then Roberto tossed a twisted loop of the rope over Diablo's nose.

Diablo's head rose high in resentment, and he burst into a faster and even more frenzied pace.

Roberto leaned low on the neck, clutching deep handfuls of the heavy white mane, rolling with the maddened animal's thundering gait.

Within an hour Diablo stopped. He stood perfectly still in a shallow arroyo, as though getting himself out of sight of any other mustangs before admitting that he had been captured.

"*Buenos días*, Señor Diablo Blanco," Roberto said softly, patting the horse on his sweat-foamed neck. "You are a brave horse. Believe me, I am very tired myself . . . . "

Chapter Seventeen

Six weeks later, on a bright cool November morning, Roberto rode the white stallion across the prairie dog desert and through the deep grass prairie to Fort Mystic. Escorted by the sentry who had challenged him outside, he entered the barricade, leading his Comanche horse and the two gentled mustangs he had used to capture Diablo.

"A visitor to see Lieutenant Greentree, Sergeant," the sentry said.

Roberto sat proudly on the white stallion and waited. Before approaching the garrison, he had stopped a mile away and brushed down the horse. He had washed his sheepskin pad at the last stream he crossed and dried it in the sun. He now used it as a saddle, and he sat erectly, hoping to make a good impression on the cavalry officers.

Presently the Lieutenant and Colonel Waycross, the garrison commander, strode from the officers' quarters, their boots glistening.

Diablo reared at the sudden sight of the uniformed men and pranced on his hind legs for several moments, walking backward as Roberto controlled him with the reins.

"Who is this?" Lieutenant Greentree asked.

"Roberto de Alverez Jones, Lieutenant. You and your troops helped me on the desert last year when my grandfather was sick with sunstroke."

"Yes, of course. You have grown a lot, Roberto—"

The lieutenant's voice broke off suddenly. His eyes were now on the white stallion. It was plain that he knew he was looking at the most remarkable animal he had ever seen.

"That—that's the famous Diablo Blanco, Colonel!" he said. "This boy has captured him!"

"I hoped you would tell me where to find your horse-buyer friend, Lieutenant. You said last year that — "

"That he would pay a thousand dollars for this horse," Lieutenant Greentree finished for him. "And he will! This is great luck for you, Roberto. My friend is going to visit the garrison some time this week." He turned to the commander and said, "Colonel Waycross, I would like to ask permission for this young man to be put up here and his horses tended until my friend arrives. This is the most remarkable stallion that has ever been captured."

"I've heard of him," the colonel answered, staring in admiration at the white horse, "and I am sure that we would all like to look this animal over. Welcome back to Fort Mystic, young man."

"Thank you, Colonel Waycross," Roberto said, sliding to the ground.

"Lieutenant," said the colonel, "dispatch a man to prepare stables."

"Yes, sir. Sergeant Baker."

"Sir."

"Instruct the stable sergeant to make room for four horses. Prepare the largest stable for Diablo Blanco."

"Yes, sir." Sergeant Baker gave a quick salute and went on the double.

Colonel Waycross said, "Trumpeter."

"Sir," said the trumpeter.

"Sound Officers' Call." He turned to the lieutenant. "I want all the officers to see this horse. He is truly magnificent."

A thrill of great pride rose in Roberto as he listened to the trumpeter blow Officers' Call. The bugle notes crackled in the crisp air, sending a special charge through the atmosphere of the garrison. Officers came running from the parade ground, the stables, and the blacksmith shop.

Roberto noticed Corporal Red Moon standing beside the barricade gates, staring at him speculatively. He could not read Red Moon's face at all, but he was sure that Red Moon would respect him for having captured the killer stallion.

"I see Corporal Red Moon over there," he said to the colonel.

"Yes." Colonel Waycross called to Red Moon. "You may join us in my office for a while, Corporal. I'm sure this lad has much to say that will interest you . . . . "

Chapter Eighteen

THE officers gathered in the colonel's office and listened as Roberto told about the death of his grandfather at the water hole. He described out of painful memory, the burial of his grandfather and the bitterness that swam in his heart toward the killer stallion. He admitted without shame that revenge had made his heart murderous.

When he reached the point in his story where he had looked down the gun sights at Diablo Blanco across the Guadalupe canyon, he paused.

"I couldn't pull the trigger, Colonel Waycross," he

said. "I . . . thought the big horse was just too beautiful to be killed."

The colonel ran fingers through his sandy-gray hair and nodded in understanding.

"You were quite right, young man. Being wild, the horse would have done anything to maintain his freedom. One can't really blame him for what he did. Mustangs will often die before accepting captivity."

"I know that. My grandfather told me."

"You must have handled Diablo well after you caught him. He seems under control, but with a good spirit in him still. How did you do it?"

"I could not throw him, and I think that may have been the saving thing, Colonel. I had to ride him into submission instead of tying and blindfolding him the way I did the others."

"Do you mean," asked Lieutenant Greentree, "that you leaped onto the back of that horse and rode him down?"

"Yes," Roberto admitted.

"How did you ever get close enough?"

"I used the other horses in relays. It took five days. That's the way my own father used to catch the tough ones, Lieutenant. I can remember him doing it."

"Well," said the lieutenant, shaking his head in wonder, "you have earned your money. I'm sure my friend will be very glad to have this stallion." He turned to Colonel Waycross. "You see, Colonel, this horse will be turned back onto the prairie with a tame herd and used for breeding stock. That's why my friend is willing to pay so much for him."

"But," said Roberto quickly, "Diablo Blanco will never stay with a tame herd more than a day or two. He will run wild again, and return to his own prairie!"

"No," said the lieutenant. "The horse-breeders will first cut a tendon in one of his hind legs and cripple him. He will never be able to run away again, even though he is loose on the prairie."

A deep sickening crawled in Roberto's stomach. He stared aghast at the lieutenant.

"Cripple him?" he asked in disbelief.

"It seems a shame," the lieutenant admitted, "but horse-breeders have to be practical. By sacrificing one great horse's ability to run, an entire herd will be upgraded. I can understand that you don't like the idea. But you'll have your reward, and you will not have to see Diablo after he has been crippled. Do you also plan to sell the other two mustangs you have gentled?"

"I . . . guess so," Roberto answered, too stunned to think clearly.

Then he heard Corporal Red Moon calling from the window of the colonel's office.

"Colonel Waycross! Smoke signals, look. To the south. Comanche war signals."

All the officers ran outside to look. Far to the south a slender column of smoke rose into the sky, with billowing puffs at irregular intervals. Red Moon stared, then looked to the north.

"There!" he pointed. "Another one. They are being relayed."

"What are they saying?" the colonel asked.

"I cannot read them, Colonel, sir," said Red Moon. "Buffalo Eaters change their smoke words from time to time. It is a war call. I think it has to do with the Kiowas. They will be moving south to winter camps soon."

Roberto watched the signals and knew immediately what they said. The Comanches had word that the Kiowas were planning to send a raiding party down on Fort Mystic as they passed through the escarpments nearby on their way south. The Comanches were calling their own war parties together to massacre the main Kiowa train. The old people, the children, and the women who were not stolen would all be killed.

As he studied the smoke signals, he noticed that Red Moon had begun watching him intently.

"You understand?" Red Moon asked after a few moments.

"N-no," Roberto stammered. He did not want the cavalry to start slaughtering Indians. Neither did he want the Kiowas to massacre the army.

"Colonel, sir! Lieutenant Greentree! This part-brown white-boy understands. He has lately been with the Buffalo Eaters."

"Why do you think that?" asked the colonel.

"One of his horses has a split ear. It is a Comanche horse. I believe this boy has been to Conas. Chief Leaning Rock was his friend, and that's where Leaning Rock's warriors are trained." Red Moon scowled and his eyes flashed like sudden lightning. "This boy knows a lot. You must make him talk."

Colonel Waycross turned slowly. He ran his fingers through his hair in that nervous way he had and stared down at Roberto with the most curious expression. There was sadness in it—and angry determination.

"Tell me what you know," he said. His words were clipped; he meant business.

"I know nothing," Roberto said. He needed time to think before he told them anything.

"You are lying, young man. The Comanches and

the Kiowas are savages. The United States Army is going to control them until they are civilized and ready to settle down on their reservations."

"And become tame, and learn how to cripple horses?" Roberto asked with anger exploding inside him. "You explained to me, Colonel, that Diablo Blanco killed to protect his freedom. You said you could not blame him. The Buffalo Eaters become savage to protect their freedom—"

"Rot!" said the colonel. "That is no comparison at all. Comanches and Kiowas kill each other just to get each other's horses and women!"

Bitterly confused Roberto said, "Diablo killed another stallion the day he killed my grandfather. I watched it. He was trying to get the mares from the other herd—"

"People are of a much higher order than horses, Roberto. At least, they should be. Perhaps you are too young to understand. I appreciate your loyalty to the Indians—obviously they are your friends. The army wants only to stop them from killing and marauding."

"Soldiers sometimes give them whiskey and then rob them, Colonel. You know very well that many soldiers and civilians cheat them every chance they have. A peddler recently tried to cheat me because

I was wearing a breechclout and he thought I was an Indian—"

"There!" cried Corporal Red Moon. "I told you he had been to Conas. He was wearing a breechclout . . . ."

Colonel Waycross thought for several moments. "Roberto," he said at last, "I assume you are an American citizen. The United States Army needs information that I have reason to believe you possess. We need that information to keep the peace on the border. I order you to give it to me."

"I do not know whether I am an American citizen or not," Roberto said. "My father was born and raised in the Arizona Territory and I was born in Mexico—"

"You are under arrest, young man," the colonel snapped. "Corporal Red Moon."

"Sir," said the corporal.

"Escort the prisoner to the guardhouse."

"Yes, sir," said Red Moon saluting.

Chapter Nineteen

FROM the guardhouse window Roberto could see the Comanche smoke signals on the northern horizon. The message being relayed was clear. Comanche war parties were to converge on a certain crest along the escarpments to the north. They would massacre the Kiowas one day very soon, but he could not yet tell from the signals which day. It would be the day, of course, that all the Kiowa warriors would attack Fort Mystic. So much bloodshed was sickening to think about.

Red Moon brought Roberto's food from the mess hall and placed it on the bench in his cell.

"Talk to me," he said urgently. "If soldiers make mistake, many people may be killed, more than necessary. Tell me what you know."

"If I could get out of here," Roberto said, "nobody would be killed."

"Why do you say that?" Red Moon's face became suspicious. (Roberto decided he did not dare take Red Moon fully into his confidence.) "The Comanches are going to raid the Kiowas. Tell me when, and the soldiers will break it up before many people die."

"Suppose," said Roberto, "a detachment of troops goes out to break up a Comanche raid and this garrison is raided while they are gone? Fort Mystic could be wiped out."

"When is this going to happen?"

"I do not know, Red Moon! I said *suppose* . . . . "

"But you know the fort is going to be attacked?"

"I do not know anything," Roberto cried, almost too confused to think. If he told them exactly what was going to happen, and studied the smoke signals until he knew exactly when—what would the troops do? They would simply prepare for two bloody defenses at once: one here where Kiowas would be slaughtered, and one over near the Kiowa train where Comanches would be slaughtered. Kill, kill, kill . . . that's all any of them ever thought about, soldiers or Indians.

If I could get out of here, he said silently to himself . . . .

Red Moon turned suddenly and left the cell, making certain that the heavy door was locked.

He returned the next morning shortly after the trumpeter had blown Reveille. The trumpeter, who was also a corporal, was with him.

They talked as they approached the guardhouse door, and Roberto could hear them.

"That boy is as wild as an animal," said the trumpeter. "I wonder when his hair was last cut? Do you think he lives with the Indians?"

"Not all the time," Red Moon answered. "He is certainly as wild as that horse. He lives on the prairies, alone."

They came through the door and announced that they were a special detail sent to escort him to the colonel's office.

"You may be court-martialed," Red Moon said with a very strange smile touching his lips.

"I am not a soldier," Roberto replied quickly. "The army cannot court-martial a civilian."

"I think," said Red Moon, "they may make an exception in your case. Come without a struggle, or we will put you in chains."

"You are trying to frighten me, that's all," Roberto said.

The two corporals marched him out of the guard-house and along the row of stables. At Diablo's stall they paused for a moment to admire the animal.

Red Moon said, "Some horse. You learned much from the Comanches at Conas, didn't you?" His face bore no suggestion of his feelings. Never, thought Roberto, had an Indian seemed more impassive. Which meant that Red Meen was deeply troubled. He would not hide his feelings so completely if he were not in great conflict inside his mind.

Diablo nickered as they stood beside the heavy rails at his stall.

"Whoa, boy," Roberto said. He saw his gear hanging on a peg at the head of the stall—where the stable hand had put it when he brushed Diablo down for the night.

"Let's go," Red Moon said. "Forward . . . march!"

"Look!" Roberto cried suddenly. He had already observed that only one guard stood at the main gate. He knew that he was taking a desperate chance, but he had to take it. When he shouted, he pointed toward the southern horizon.

"Where?" asked Red Moon and the trumpeter together.

"There. More smoke signals!"

The two soldiers looked to the south just long enough. Roberto sprang toward the stall, lifting down the two top rails. Grabbing his gear and a rope, he leaped upon Diablo's back.

The horse reared and jumped the remaining rails, almost raking Roberto off against the top of the stall opening.

"Hey!" shouted the trumpeter. "He's getting away!"

"Don't shoot," Red Moon cried. "Capture him— we need information from him."

Diablo reared toward the soldiers, threatening them with poised hoofs.

"Look out!" Red Moon shouted.

Roberto clutched fistfuls of the long mane and tugged on Diablo's neck, all the while digging heels into the horse's flanks. Diablo surged forward toward the main gate.

Roberto threw a loop over the horse's head as they reached the barricade. The guard raised his rifle.

"Halt!" he demanded.

But the guard had never encountered anything as fast as Diablo Blanco. The white stallion reared at him pawing the gun from his hands before he realized what was happening, and the soldier ran for his life.

Holding the rope, Roberto sprang to the ground, swung the huge log latch from the gate, and pushed it open. With another quick bound, he leaped astride Diablo again, and headed toward the escarpments to the west. A fierce pounding was in his breast.

The big stallion's hoofs made almost as much noise as an entire herd of mustangs. Soldiers gathered quickly at the main gate of the garrison but all they could see was dust rising up from the grass.

Chapter Twenty

Roberto reached the escarpments before dark and camped for the night on a low rim near the base of a notched mountain. He could see far across the plains to the north, east, and south. He watched for smoke signals at daybreak the next morning. There were none. That probably meant that this would be the day of the attack.

"Diablo," he said, "the Kiowa train will never travel along the edge of the escarpments, for this is too near the Comanche Trail. They will travel by night, staying in the deepest grass possible, and camp out of sight during the daytime."

The horse, tied to a mesquite tree, munched on a clump of tall bunch grass. He laid back his ears at the sound of his name and Roberto had to laugh aloud.

"So . . . you know your name. You are a very smart horse. You did a fine job helping me get past that barricade yesterday. I will never sell you to become a cripple, Diablo . . . ."

All morning he searched the prairie for signs of the troops from Fort Mystic. But all he could see was an ocean of brown grass undulating in the November breeze. As he watched and waited, he made his plan.

He spent the afternoon twisting dry grass into tightly tied hanks the size of a fist. He stuffed the hanks into all his pockets and into a bag he made of a shirt.

He found a dry soapberry stump, broke a knot from it, and charred the knot in his fire. At dusk he tied the charred knot and the bag of twisted grass to his horse and rode down to the prairie. His breast again pounded with anticipation.

He took a careful bearing from the notch above him just before dark and then moved by starlight four or five miles down a long incline on the prairie toward Fort Mystic. He searched for a high place and stationed himself there, as nearly as possible on a line between the fort and the notch from which he had taken his bearing. Then he waited all night.

The November moon was late. Rising finally, it rode high in the cool breeze. Tonight it was barely on the wane, providing plenty of light for him to see any mass movement in the grass.

Just before dawn the Kiowas came, exactly as he thought they would. They rode from the west, silently. He could see their dark shapes—a hundred of them at least—moving in a long line down the prairie slope.

"All right, Diablo," he whispered, "we must make this work."

He dropped to the ground and built a small quick fire in the grass, lighting the charred soapberry knot for a torch. The wind pushed up the flame from his fire and the prairie began to burn.

Leaping onto his horse, he rode straight across the path of the approaching Kiowas. He lit the twisted hanks of grass with his torch and threw them into tall clumps on the prairie as he rode.

The wind was helpful. It picked up the flames in a hurry. Soon a line of fire stretched out behind him as though the prairie were the sky and he a blazing comet.

He could hear the Kiowas yelling as they turned to flee back up the slope from the flames.

"It's working, Diablo," he said, riding as hard as he could, "Now we must reach the escarpments before the Comanches attack."

He urged Diablo hard and the big horse responded with heroic speed. Within minutes he could see the notch in the horizon by moonlight.

Choosing a line that he thought would cut off the Comanches from the Kiowa train, he started his fire trail again. Diablo took him furiously toward the notch. He threw out blazing hanks of twisted grass as fast as he could light them.

By the time he reached the base of the mountain, he could hear the Comanche cries—the war whoops and the Indian curses. He had cut them off, and they now fled back toward the south whence they had come.

"Diablo," he said, with a mixture of joy and sadness in his heart, "there will be no bloodshed tonight. The Kiowas will be sorry, the Comanches will be sorry, and I am sure the troops will be sorry when they figure out what happened."

If people used as much imagination to prevent warfare as they spent waging it, he thought, remembering the colonel's words, *they might indeed be of a higher order than animals.*

"Not that I intend to insult you," he said, petting his horse's neck. "But you have accepted captivity. Human beings never will."

When dawn broke over the blackened prairie, Roberto sat astride his proud white stallion and looked down from the rim on the edge of the mountain, below the notch.

"My grandfather once told me," he explained to Diablo, "that burning a prairie sometimes makes it grow back thicker than ever."

Then, as the sun rose, he turned to the west, thinking about his camp on the high mesa near the prairie basin above the Guadalupe. He hoped no one had found his little corral in the box canyon.

"You will like it, Diablo," he said. "The grass there is very tall . . . . "